What I Want to Be

written by Mark A. Taylor
illustrated by Dick Wahl

Library of Congress Catalog Card No. 85-62959
© 1986. The STANDARD PUBLISHING Company, Cincinnati, Ohio
Division of STANDEX INTERNATIONAL Corporation. Printed in U.S.A.

Each time I go to my church,
  There's a nice man that I meet
Before I even get inside
  To go to class or find a seat.

He's standing at the front door.
"Come in," he'll smile and say.

"How good it is to see you!
How are you folks today?"

He bends to shake my hand,
  And knows my name is Tim.
Someday I'd like to be a greeter
  Just like him.

And then I go to my class
　And meet my teacher there.
She also calls me by my name,
　Then shows me to a chair.

"What should we do today, Tim?
   I know we'll have some fun.
We'll color a picture, and play a game,
   And learn about God's Son."

Then she tells a Bible story,
  When everyone is there.
Someday I'll be a teacher
  Just like her.

Sometimes I go to "big church"
   And sit with Mother and Dad.
I take some books along and write
   With pencils on a pad.

I hear the pretty music
  And sometimes sing along.
And usually I listen
  When the choir sings its song.

And as I watch the leader
  Wave his arms to lead each hymn,
I think I'd like to be a singer
  Just like him.

Sometimes I like to listen
  When the preacher stands to speak.
"He helps us," Daddy tells me,
  "To live for God all week."

I know my parents listen, too,
   Because I'm watching them.
Someday I'd like to be a preacher
   Just like him.

These aren't the only people
Who help us when we're ther
Some men take up the offering

And others say a prayer.

Some read from the Bible.

Some help us find a seat.

Some help take attendance.

Some fix good things to eat!

And as I see each person at church,
I pray and say, "God, please,
Help me to be a leader someday
Just like these."